God Knows My Name

Written and illustrated by **Debby Anderson**

"Hi! My name is Mario."

CROSSWAY

WHEATON, ILLINOIS

Dear Grown-up Readers,

Unimaginable . . . the God of the universe knows our names! His Word tells us so. The biblical references are included for your own study. Enjoy discovering the reality of God's omniscient care for you, too.

Prayerfully,

Debby Anderson

Gratefully acknowledging: Rob Erdle,
Regents Professor of Watercolor at the University of North Texas

---

God Knows My Name

Text and illustrations copyright © 2003 by Debby Anderson
Published by Crossway
        1300 Crescent Street
        Wheaton, Illinois 60187 USA

First printing 2003
Printed in Singapore

ISBN-13: 978-1-58134-415-8
ISBN-10: 1-58134-415-5
PDF ISBN: 978-1-4335-2904-7
Mobipocket ISBN: 978-1-4335-2905-4
ePub ISBN: 978-1-4335-2906-1

Library of Congress Cataloging-in-Publication Data
Anderson, Debby.
   God knows my name / written and illustrated by Debby Anderson.
     p.   cm.
   Summary: Explains how God knows, sees, and cares for everything in the world.
   ISBN 13: 978-1-58134-415-8 (tpb : alk. paper)
   ISBN 10: 1-58134-415-5
   1. God—Omniscience—Juvenile literature. [1. God.] I. Title.
BT131.A43   2003
231'.4—dc21   2002007471

Crossway is a publishing ministry of Good News Publishers.

IM		24	23	22	21	20	19	18	17	16	15	14	13
21	20	19	18	17	16	15	14	13	12	11	10	9	8

To my kindergarten class
(who wrote their names inside this book's cover)
and to all the terrific students and staff
at Tisinger Elementary!
Lovingly,
Mrs. Anderson

God made everything and
God knows everything! God knows me.
He even knows my favorite color.
What's your favorite color? Surprise!
God already knew it!

Psalm 139:1

Katie

Sy'kia

God knows my name!
He even knows how many
hairs are on my head.

Top

Ahmed

Trevor

Jill

Elena

Can you count how many hairs are on your head? What is your name?

Matthew 10:30; John 10:3

Tyrone

Before God made the world, He knew about me.
Before I was born, God knew what would happen
every day of my life....

Ephesians 1:4; Psalm 139:15-16

My surprise birthday party didn't even surprise God! Nothing surprises God! God sees me when I sit down or when I stand up.

Psalm 139:2-3

On the first day of school, when no one knows my name yet, God knows my name! He hears every thought I think and every word I say.

Psalm 139:2, 4, 23

God sees me when I go out to play! Yay!
God is too wonderful for me to see Him now,
but He sees me!

Psalm 139:3

God sees me when I go to bed. He can watch over me because He never sleeps. He can see in the dark!

God sends out the stars at night and wakes up the sun in the morning.

Psalm 139:3, 12; 121:3; Job 38:12,32

When I hide in my favorite hiding place,
God can find me! Nothing can hide from God!
Even if I float far across the ocean, God knows.
He tells the waves where to stop!

He's touched the very bottom of the sea!
Can you find the crab, octopus, starfish, snail,
anemone, sea slug, and jellyfish?

Hebrews 4:13; Psalm 139:9; Job 38:8-11, 16

God understands how horses run and eagles fly!
When the lion cubs are hungry, God helps their
family find food. God helps us, too.
Thank You, God, for our food.

Job 38:39; 39:19, 27

God can count every star up in space.
He put every one in its place! Just as He
knows my name, He knows every star's name!

Psalm 147:4; Isaiah 40:26; Job 38:2

God knows how to send the snow, frost, wind...

...lightning, thunder, rain...and dew!

Job 38:22-30, 34

When a deer has her baby, God knows!
When a sparrow falls to the ground,
or when I fall to the ground, God knows!
He always knows how I feel.

Job 39:1; Matthew 10:29; Hebrews 4:15-16

God understands when I feel sad, glad, mad, or bad!

He cares when I feel confident or embarrassed, scared or excited!

2 Corinthians 1:3-4; Isaiah 53:4; 1 Chronicles 28:9

God knows the names of everyone in the whole wide world! And I want everyone everywhere to know God! So day and night, I'll make music and sing and talk about His name!

Psalms 92:1-2; 147:5

"O Lord . . .
I will give glory
to your name
forever, for
you love me
so much!"

Psalm 86:5, 12 TLB

"¡Adios, amigos!"